THE
HALLOWEEN PARTY
FROM THE
BLACK LAGOON

THE
HALLOWEEN PARTY
FROM THE
BLACK LAGOON

by Mike Thaler

Illustrated by Jared Lee

SCHOLASTIC INC.

New York   Toronto   London   Auckland   Sydney
Mexico City   New Delhi   Hong Kong   Buenos Aires

To Tom and Suzanne
—M.T.

In memory of:
Eddie Stanley, Jr.
February 21, 1998

My best buddy ever.
—J.L.

ISBN 0-439-68075-1

Text copyright © 2004 by Mike Thaler.
Illustrations copyright © 2004 by Jared D. Lee Studio, Inc.

48 47 46 45 44 43 42 41 40   15 16 17/0

Printed in the U.S.A.
First printing, October 2004

CONTENTS

CHAPTER 1
HALLO-WHEN?

Mrs. Green says that we're going to have a Halloween party at school. Next *Fright-day*, we all have to come to class in costumes. Then we'll all vote and pick the best one. Mrs. Green says there's a totally awesome first prize.

I have no idea who or what I should come as. Maybe I should just stay home that day and come as the Invisible Man.

ARF
ARF
ARF

CHAPTER 2
DISGUISE THE LIMIT

On the school bus, all the kids are excited about their costumes. Eric says he has a beautiful rubber mask. The eyeball is hanging out and there's an ax stuck in the brain. Needless to say, there's lots of fake blood on it.

THIS IS SO COOL.

The girls are not impressed. Penny says there's an ax stuck in Eric's brain all the time, and that she may come as a princess. Eric says he'll be happy to crown her.

PLEASE BOW.

Doris waves her arm and says that she's coming as a ballet dancer. The boys are not at all impressed.

Freddy is coming as a werewolf—claws and all. Eric says he should come as an *underwear-wolf*. Randy is coming as Count Dracula. He says it's a disguise you can really sink your teeth into.

IM A SWAN.

WEIRDWOLF

BURP.

FULL MOON

UNDERWEAR-WOLF

WHAT IS DRACULA'S FAVORITE FRUIT?

ANSWER ON PAGE 22.

11

And Derek is coming as a mummy.

Eric says, "Why not come as a daddy? And what about you, Hubie?"

"Me . . . oh, my costume's still in the planning stage," I reply. The truth is, I have no idea what I will come as. I'm having an identity crisis!

I'M ALL WRAPPED UP IN MY COSTUME.

CHAPTER 3
GO FOR BROKE!

When I get home, I empty my piggy bank, but there's not a lot in it. I'm able to shake out $2.38. This is not good.

I don't have high hopes as I get on my bike and pedal toward the costume shop. When I arrive, it's monster mayhem!

13

Every aisle is fiend-filled.
Blood and guts galore. It's like
going to the movies. Every
major monster is there—
Frankenstein, Dracula, Wolfman,
and the Thing. It's all fur, fangs,
blood, and bolts.

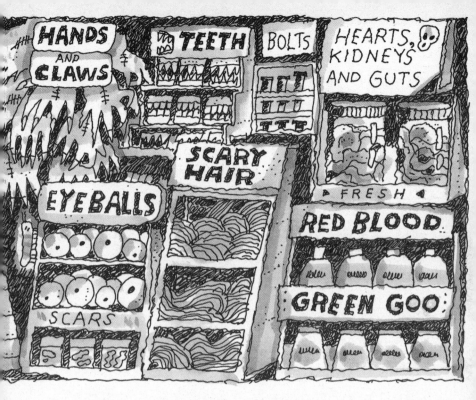

Everything looks really cool. The only problem is the price tags are monstrous, too. There's nothing less than thirty dollars. Even the masks are all more than ten dollars. I recount my money. It's not $2.38. It's $2.37.

The saleswoman isn't very helpful. She just says to go look on the sale rack by the door. Well, there's a scar for $2.99, an eyeball for $3.99, a set of fangs for $4.99, and a tube that squirts fake blood for $5.99.

← NOODLE →

I open my hand and look at my $2.37. I can afford one Martian antenna or one witch's wart, but that's not going to make a great costume. I'm going to have to look elsewhere.

OPEN

THE MONSTER COSTUME SHOP

AND CAFE

ENTER AT YOUR OWN RISK

BRAINS FOR SALE

KING KONG

16

← SPIDERS

17

CHAPTER 4
A HOME REMEDY

As I slouch on the couch, Mom comes over and sits down next to me. "What's the matter?" she asks.

I tell her about the Halloween party, the contest, and my costume problem. She smiles, takes my hand, and leads me up to the attic. There she opens an old trunk and pulls out a cardboard crown.

ATTIC

I WONDER IF IT WILL STILL FIT?
TEXAS
OLD TEETH
PHOTOS
PHOTOS
$1.96
FRANCE
MOM'S PROM DRESS (NEVER USED)
CALIFORNIA
OHIO
AUNT BETTY'S JAM 1968

"When I was a little girl, we didn't have much money either," she smiles while putting on the crown. "So I just made my own costumes, like this princess costume." She straightens two of the crown's droopy points.

"That's a great idea, Mom," I say as she looks in the mirror.

WHAT DO YOU CALL A MONSTER WHO HAS A BABY? ANSWER: PAGE 29

21

She skipped back to the trunk and pulled out a big pink eraser cap. "Another year, I was a number two pencil," she winks while putting on the cap. "It was a pretty *sharp* costume."

"I get the *point*, Mom, but I don't know *what* to be," I sigh.

"Just use your imagination, Hubie." She smiles, pats me on the shoulder, and goes back downstairs as an eraser head.

A DINER-SAUR

EAT

OPEN

ANSWER: A NECK-TARINE

23

CHAPTER 5
A SCREAM OF A DREAM

That night, I have one crazy dream. I'm at school, but my whole class is full of monsters . . . *real* monsters! They all have a hard time fitting into their desks, especially the Blob.

Finally, they get settled down, and Mrs. Green calls the roll.

Frankenstein raises his hand and it falls off.

"I'm here, here, and here," says the Blob.

And Dracula pulls the witch's hair, so she turns him into a bloodhound.

I just sit there as quiet as can be.

"We're going to have a party for Halloween," says Mrs. Green.

All of the monsters start fidgeting in their desks. They're all worried about their costumes. Frankenstein says he may come as Elvis.

STAY OFF OF MY PLATFORM SHOES.

DIG IT.

YOU ROCK.

STOMP! STOMP! STOMP!

26

Dracula thinks he may be a nurse from the blood bank. And the Wolfman may dress up as a schnauzer.

I tell the witch that she could be a pencil, and the Blob that he could be a Brussels sprout. They all look at me. "And what are you going to be, Hubie?" they all ask.

Luckily, I wake up before I have to answer them. I just stare up at the ceiling. I don't even see the distant glimmer of an idea. I think my imagination still must be sleeping.

CHAPTER 6
CLOTHES ENCOUNTERS

The next day, I go to the library in search of inspiration. Mrs. Beamster gives me a book on costumes.

Boy, people sure used to dress funny. They didn't always wear baseball caps and sneakers. They wore tunics, tights, sandals, and bedsheets!

← MRS. BEAMSTER, THE LIBRARIAN.

ANSWER: A MOMSTER

I wonder if in a hundred years our clothes will look as funny to future folks.

Mrs. Beamster says that in other parts of the world, even today, people dress differently than we do.

I could wear my bathrobe and be a sheik, or I could be Santa Claus, or even a submarine. Whoa, now my imagination has finally woken up—I'm on my way!

KING HUBIE

HO HO HO

HUBIE CLAUS

DIVE! DIVE!

ARF ARF

HU-BOAT

SUB

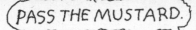

CHAPTER 7
THE PICK OF
THE GLITTER

Well, now the problem is I have too many ideas! I could make a big bun out of pillows and be a hot dog. Maybe I could put a pillow on my head and be a marshmallow.

I could draw a dial on my belly and be a cell phone. I could even cut a window in a box, draw a keyboard, and be a computer. Or I could get between two pieces of cardboard and be a book. There's so much to be!

33

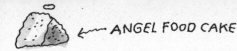

On my way home from school, all the possibilities are parading in my mind. Then we pass a billboard with an angel on it. Hmmm, an angel? That's it! I'll be an angel. I'm on cloud nine.

34

GOLD
PAINT
(SHAKE
WELL)

CHAPTER 8
WINGING IT!

COAT HANGER (WIRE NOT WOOD)

At home, I get to work. I take a wire coat hanger and bend it into a halo. It's easy—a little circle on top and a bigger circle on the bottom that fits on my head. It looks a little like a TV antenna, so I spray it with gold paint.

PLIERS
(ASK MOM
FOR HELP)

MAKING A
HALO
WHAT YOU NEED

COOL

Wings—how am I going to make those? Two pillows don't work. Two paper plates look lame. Mom says to get some cardboard and she'll help me cut out wings. Mom is a good artist. She draws me a pair of wings. Then I cut them out, but they still look like they are made of cardboard.

PILLOWS- **NO!**

WINGS

GLOVES- **NO!**

PAPER PLATES- **NO!**

TENNIS RACKETS- **NO!**

PLASTIC MILK BOTTLES- **NO!**

"Bummer," I sigh.

Suddenly, out of nowhere, Mom yells out, "Feathers! We need lots of feathers."

We both look at Peeper, our parakeet. No-ooo way! Peeper needs all the feathers he's got.

"Hmmm. Let's try the park," says Mom.

We drive over, but the pigeons want to keep all theirs, too.

So we rush over to the market. But we're out of *pluck*. All the chickens are already naked.

"Pillows!" shouts Mom. "What was I thinking?! Pillows are full of feathers. And we have lots of those at home."

39

We speed home and find an old down pillow. Mom opens it up and shakes it out. Now we are in fine feather weather.

Feathers float and fall all over the room like snowflakes.

Mom and I catch them in midair and glue them to the wings. Now they look like they belong to an angel. I'm almost ready to fly!

CHAPTER 9
THE BIG DAY!

It's Friday morning, and it's the big day—Halloween party time! I am so excited I can't stop moving.

I start to get ready. I put on a white T-shirt and my white bathing suit. Mom puts my wings on my back with duct tape. Easy as pie!

I put on my halo and look in the mirror. There was even some cardboard left over and I made a little cloud. I look cool—simply heavenly.

CLOUD NINE →

CHAPTER 10
HALLOWEEN SCENE

When the school bus pulls up, it looks like it just came from the cemetery. Eric's eyeball is swinging back and forth. And instead of a hat . . . he's wearing a *hat-chet*! Gross!

Freddy's got on rubber claws, and he's trying to pick his nose. Even more gross!

Penny decided to be a witch. I recognize her $1.99 wart. She's casting spells on Derek to turn him into a frog. But he's wrapped in toilet paper and already beginning to unwind.

Randy is Count Dracula. He's got the $4.99 fangs and a cape. Doris is dressed in her tutu and ballet shoes. She looks a lot like a dancer.

I have to stand up all the way to school because I don't want to bend my wings.

44

CHAPTER 11
PARTY ANIMALS

Mrs. Green has done an awesome job decorating our classroom. It looks like a real swamp.

There are big black spiders with crepe paper legs—wiggling on the walls. Jack-o'-lanterns with candles are glowing in the corner. And striped snakes made from toilet paper tubes are rolling around on the floor.

There are lots of funny signs like: LOOK OUT FOR ALLIGATORS!; WELCOME GHASTLY GHOSTS AND GRUESOME GHOULS FROM GRISLY GRAVES!; and CREEPY CRAWLING CROSSING!

Mrs. Green is in a cool costume, too. She's dressed like a baseball player. She has a uniform, a cap, and a bat.

We all sit at our desks and she takes attendance. "Wolfman?"

"Here," says Freddy, raising his paw.

"Mr. Eyeball Hatchet Head?"

"Here," says Eric, swinging his orb.

47

Mrs. Green continues to do the roll call.

"Count Dracula?"

"Heeeere," shouts Randy, as he chomps his fangs.

"Miss Witch?"

"I'm here," squeals Penny, wiggling her fingers.

"Mummy?"

"Here," moans Derek, still unwinding down the aisle.

"Prima Ballerina?"

"Here," sings Doris, raising her arm to look like a swan.

"And our Angel?"

"Here," I say, trying to flap my wings.

Big mistake. A flutter of feathers fills the room.

"Well, we're all here," says Mrs. Green as she closes her attendance book. "And how wonderful you all look."

Eric swivels his eyeball around to survey the room. "Now, let's have our contest. Come up front, one at a time, and tell us a little about your costume. Penny, you'll be first," says Mrs. Green, pointing her bat.

← INVISIBLE BOY

BATBOY ←

CHAPTER 12
SHARING WHAT YOU'RE WEARING

Penny sails up on a broom to the front of the class. "I'm a witch, and you're all going to be frogs," she says, wiggling her fingers.

"Which witch are you?" shouts Derek.

"I'm the *sand-witch* in the kitchen," proclaims Penny as she floats back to her seat.

Derek's next. He unwinds all the way up to the front. "I'm a mummy, and I'm two thousand years old."

"You don't look a day over one thousand," yells Eric.

"Watch what you're saying, Eric," says Mrs. Green.

Eric puts his dangling eyeball into his mouth.

I'M A COOL GHOUL.

"I live in a state of *deNile*," smiles Derek.

"Time to wrap it up," says Mrs. Green.

"Okay. Knock, knock," says Derek.

"Who's there?" asks everyone.

"Mummified," smiles Derek.

"Mummified who?" we ask.

"My mummified me a yummy hamburger for lunch today," laughs Derek.

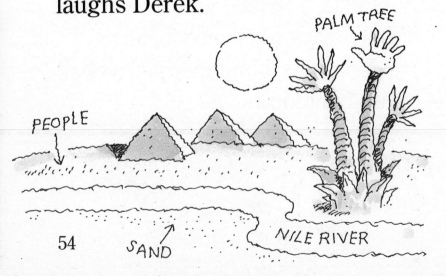

54

Eric's next. "How about a *hand-burger,*" says Eric, pulling off his fake hand. I hope he doesn't give me a hand with anything.

He opens up his shirt and all his intestines fall out. YUCK! At least it's not lunchtime yet.

"You've certainly got a lot of guts," smiles Mrs. Green. I love when teachers make jokes.

Soon Doris spins down the aisle, twirls, and bows.

Then Freddy bounds up and raises his paws. "A poem," he starts to recite. "Does a werewolf wear underwear underneath all his hair?"

"I'm unaware, but I am next," I answer as I fly up front in a flurry of feathers. And I almost lose my halo.

"I'm an angel," I smile, straightening my halo.

"Just remember that for the rest of the year," smiles Mrs. Green. I hate it when teachers make jokes.

59

Randy's last. He slinks up front. "Allow me to *entrodouth* myself. I am Count Dracula from Transylvania."

"You need a *Transyl-fusion*," shouts Eric.

"Eric, please pull yourself together," says Mrs. Green.

"I'm a little batty," continues Randy as he holds up his cape and flaps back to his seat.

"Well, you all look beautiful," says Mrs. Green. "But we have to pick a winner for the grand prize."

VERY NICE, KIDS.

WHAT IS DRACULA'S
FAVORITE HOLIDAY?
ANSWER: PAGE 62

"What *is* the grand prize?" asks Eric, snapping his eyeball.

"The grand prize is a $35 gift certificate to the costume shop," says Mrs. Green, twirling her bat.

After a lot of "oohs" and "ahs," the class votes. It's really close because all my classmates vote for themselves.

But do you know who wins? I do.

I have two votes. Someone else voted for me. As I look around the room, Eric winks his eyeball.

What a buddy! I'm going to share the grand prize with him. I'll get him a rubber heart that he can wear on his sleeve.

As for me, I've got everything I want. Angels don't need much. Well, maybe I'll just get a little harp.